SENSES

Did you know?

Everyone's body has its own particular smell, even identical twins.

We use our tongues to taste but butterflies taste with their feet.

If you have an ear infection, you may find it harder to stay balanced.

Written by Dr Patricia Macnair

Illustrated by Richard Watson

Book Band: Gold

Adapted from *Sensational Senses*,
first published in Great Britain 2015

Senses first published in Great Britain 2016 by Red Shed,
an imprint of Egmont UK Limited
The Yellow Building, 1 Nicholas Road, London W11 4AN

www.egmont.co.uk

ISBN 978 1 4052 8041 9

A CIP catalogue record for this book is available from The British Library.

Printed in China
60655/1

Series and book banding consultant: Nikki Gamble

SENSES

RED SHED

Contents

Introduction

The world we live in is a big, busy and interesting place. To make the most of it we use our senses. Our main senses are sight, hearing, taste, touch, smell and balance.

Welcome to the park

We use our senses every day. Are you ready to discover all about them at the Sensational Theme Park?

What senses can you see
being used on these pages?

Entrance

We also use our senses
to **communicate** with
each other. You can
see and hear when
someone is angry,
sad, scared or happy.

Our senses are always switched on,
even when we are asleep.

Sensors and the brain

Our brains use our senses to find out about the world around us. From our nose to our toes, every bit of a body is packed with special **sensors**.

brain

nerves

Signals from the sensors travel along **nerves** to take information to the brain.

Our brains work out what these signals mean.
Different parts of the brain have different jobs.

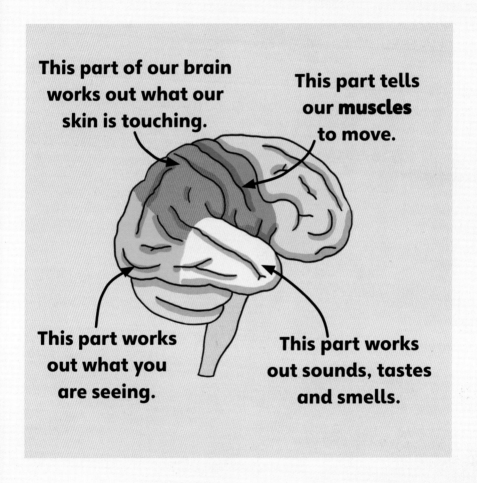

This part of our brain
works out what our
skin is touching.

This part tells
our **muscles**
to move.

This part works
out what you
are seeing.

This part works
out sounds, tastes
and smells.

Hearing

Every day, our ears pick up hundreds of different sounds. Our sense of hearing helps us communicate with each other and warns us of danger.

The loudness of a sound is measured in decibels (dB). The higher the decibels, the louder the noise.

The world record for the loudest scream is 129 decibels!

Shouting is about 70 decibels.

A whisper is about 20 decibels.

How do we hear things?

Sounds are made when the air shakes or vibrates. These waves of vibrations travel through the air to your ears.

This is how you hear:

1. The outer ear catches sounds.

2. The sounds travel down the ear canal and rattle the ear drum.

3. The rattling ear drum then shakes three tiny **bones** called the hammer, the anvil and the stirrup. This creates ripples in the liquid in the inner ear.

4. The ripples are turned into sound signals. These signals are then sent along the nerves to the brain.

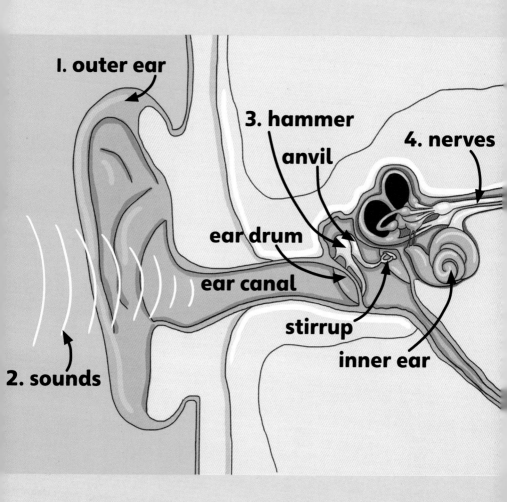

1. outer ear

3. hammer

anvil

4. nerves

ear drum

ear canal

2. sounds

stirrup

inner ear

Sight

Sight is one of the most useful senses. It helps us learn a lot about the world around us.

Many people wear glasses to help them to see.

We use our eyes to see things. They are made up of lots of important parts. Let's find out what they are and what they do.

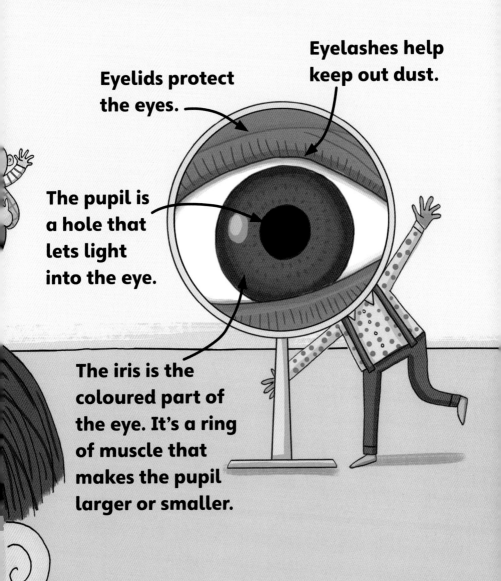

Eyelids protect the eyes.

Eyelashes help keep out dust.

The pupil is a hole that lets light into the eye.

The iris is the coloured part of the eye. It's a ring of muscle that makes the pupil larger or smaller.

15

How do we see things?

Your brain learns a lot about the world from information gathered by your eyes. This is how you see things:

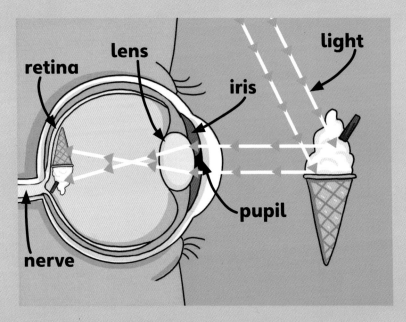

I. Light travels from an object into the eye.

2. The **lens** bends light to form an upside-down picture on the **retina**.

3. Sensors turn this picture into electrical signals that are sent along the nerve to the brain.

4. The brain turns the signals into a picture and works out what you can see.

Many people wear glasses because their eyeballs are too long or too short to focus light exactly on the retina. Lenses in glasses correct this.

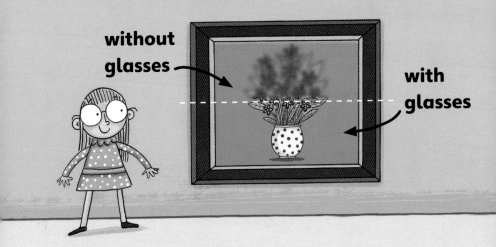

without glasses

with glasses

Some people have colour blindness. This means that they cannot tell the difference between certain colours. Most commonly, people with colour blindness muddle up reds and greens, and so wouldn't see the number 5 in the picture below.

Balance

Every time we move and even when we are standing still, we use our sense of balance. We would fall over without it! To help us balance, our brain uses information from our ears, eyes, skin, muscles and bones.

Your body may be using
hundreds of muscles to balance
itself at any one time.

If you stand on one leg and close your
eyes, you may feel much more wobbly.
This is because you have stopped using
your eyes to help you balance.

Birds use their tail feathers
to balance when they
perch on a branch.

How do we balance?

Your ears help you to balance. Deep inside them are tiny tubes and bags full of liquid called balance canals.

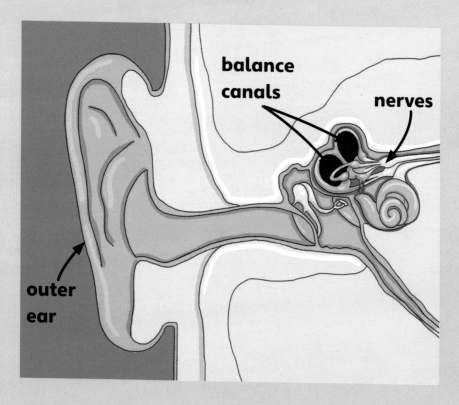

balance canals

nerves

outer ear

If you wobble around, the liquid sloshes about, sending signals to your brain about the direction you are moving in. Your brain then moves your muscles to balance your body.

Feeling dizzy

Rides can make us feel dizzy. This is because the liquid in our balance canals still sloshes about for a while, even when the ride stops. This confuses the brain and makes it hard to balance!

Moving around in different directions can make you feel sick.

Smell and taste

It's hard to resist the smell of popcorn or the taste of ice cream but these senses also warn us of dangers, such as a smoky fire.

This ice cream is yummy!

Our noses can detect at least one trillion different smells.

Your tongue helps you to taste things and it also works as a touch sensor. It detects heat, cold, **pressure**, **texture** and pain, and it helps to grip food during chewing.

23

How do we smell things?

Smells are made of tiny, invisible **chemicals** that float in the air. When you breathe them in through your nose, they land on sensors. These sensors send signals about the smell along the nerve to your brain.

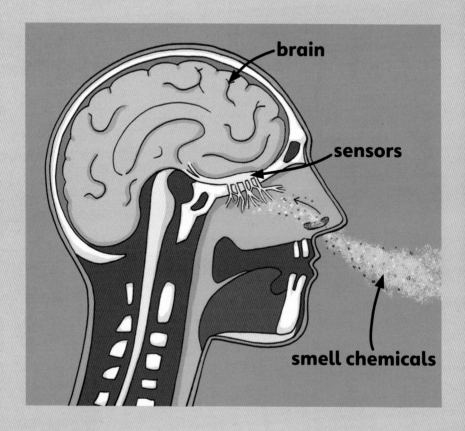

brain

sensors

smell chemicals

How do we taste things?

Your tongue is covered with thousands of sensors (called taste buds). These detect chemicals in food and drink and then send messages about the taste to your brain.

Taste buds detect five main types of taste: sweet, salty, sour, bitter and umami (a savoury flavour).

The flavour of food depends on taste and smell working together. Smell is more important so if your nose is blocked by a cold, it is difficult to taste food.

Touch

We feel our way through the world using our touch sensors. Close your eyes and touch the objects around you. Feel how cold, hard, smooth or furry they are!

Your fingertips are one of the most sensitive parts of your body.

The feel of slimy things, such as a slug or octopus, make most people squeal. Your brain is trying to protect you from danger because rotten food and other harmful things are often slimy.

BEWARE!

Your lips and tongue are full of touch sensors.

Pain is an important touch sense. It helps to protect us from danger.

Your skin is packed with thousands of special sensors that detect many different sensations.

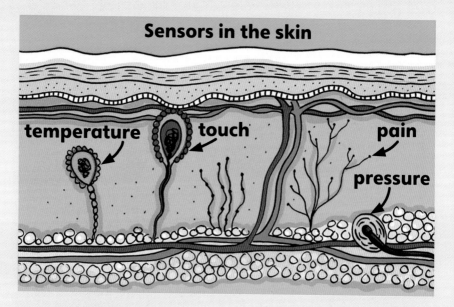

Sensors in the skin

temperature   touch   pain   pressure

Temperature sensors in your skin tell you how hot or cold something is. This warns you about very cold objects that could freeze you, or very hot objects that could burn you.

Ouch!

If you touch a sharp point, your pain sensors quickly send messages to your muscles to move away. This warning system helps you to escape from serious injury.

Pressure sensors tell us about the texture of things. If an object pushes on the skin and bends the sensors, they tell the brain the object is hard. Other types of pressure sensor react to soft things that gently stroke the skin.

Your brain uses all your senses together, especially eyesight, to work out what you are touching. If you cannot see what is tickly or squishy, your brain imagines you are touching something scary. In the dark, a fabric ghost could feel tickly, like little insects.

Fun facts

We constantly shed the top layer of our skin. Dust is mostly made of these dead skin cells.

Your ears never stop growing!

Many people have tiny creatures, called mites, living in their eyelashes. They are less than 0.5 millimetres long so you need a microscope to see them. Don't worry, they are harmless!

eyelash mite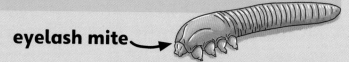

Glossary

bones Parts of the body made from hard tissue that together form your skeleton.

chemicals *(keh-mi-cals)* Substances such as water. Everything is made of chemicals, including you.

communicate To share information by speaking, writing or signalling.

lens A see-through structure inside the eye that focuses light on to the retina.

muscles *(muss-ulls)* Parts of the body that can tighten or relax to produce movement.

nerves Long, thin structures that carry signals around the body, to and from the brain.

pressure A physical force that pushes on something.

retina A layer inside the back of the eyeball that detects light coming into the eye.

sensors A structure that detects things in the world around it, such as heat, and then sends a signal to the brain about it.

signals Information sent from one place to another.

texture The feel of something.

Index